ENGIE BENJY

Job Swap

Adapted from the original episode by Bridget Appleby

Engie Benjy   **Jollop**   **Dan**

One morning Engie Benjy, Jollop and Dan were having their breakfast.

Suddenly, Tractor's picture flashed on the alarm board.

"Look!" shouted Engie, "Tractor's in trouble! Let's go, team!"

Just as they were setting off, Bus's picture flashed too.

"Whoah!" cried Engie, "Looks like Tractor and Bus need us at the same time! Come on!

THIS IS AN EMERGENCY!"

Farmer Fred climbed onto Tractor.

"Arrr! Doin' Bus's job – Easy Peasy!" said Fred, and set off to look for some passengers.

Driver Dottie and Bus drove to Farmer Fred's fields.

"We'll show 'em, eh Bus?" said Dottie, happily.

"Doing Tractor's job – easy!"

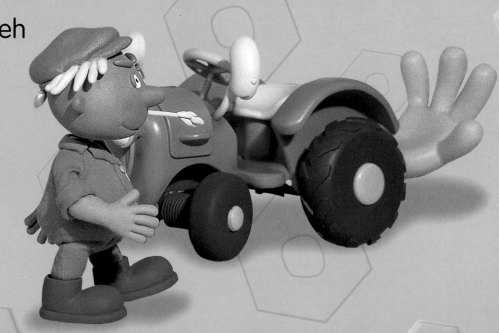

Driver Dottie found that doing Tractor's job was not easy.

First, Bus burst all the balloons in the balloon field, then he got stuck by the iced bun trees. Dottie had to push him back on to the road!

… And doing Bus's job wasn't easy either.

Astronaut Al, Pilot Pete, Fisherman Fin and Messenger Mo were all waiting at the bus stop, but Farmer Fred had lost his way.

He didn't know where the bus stop was, so all his passengers had to chase after him!

"STOP, STOP!"
they shouted.

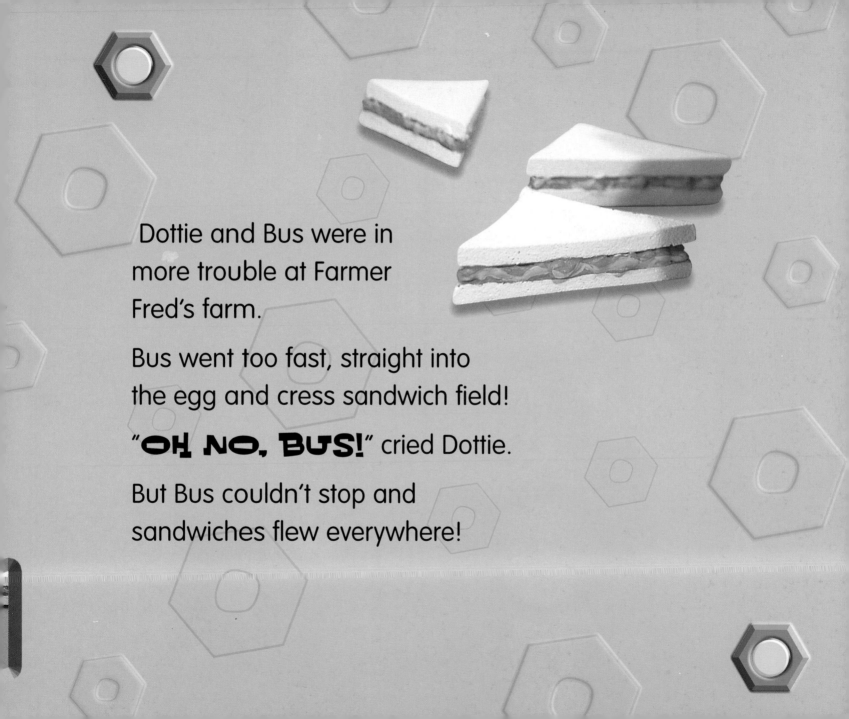

Dottie and Bus were in
more trouble at Farmer
Fred's farm.

Bus went too fast, straight into
the egg and cress sandwich field!

"OH NO, BUS!" cried Dottie.

But Bus couldn't stop and
sandwiches flew everywhere!

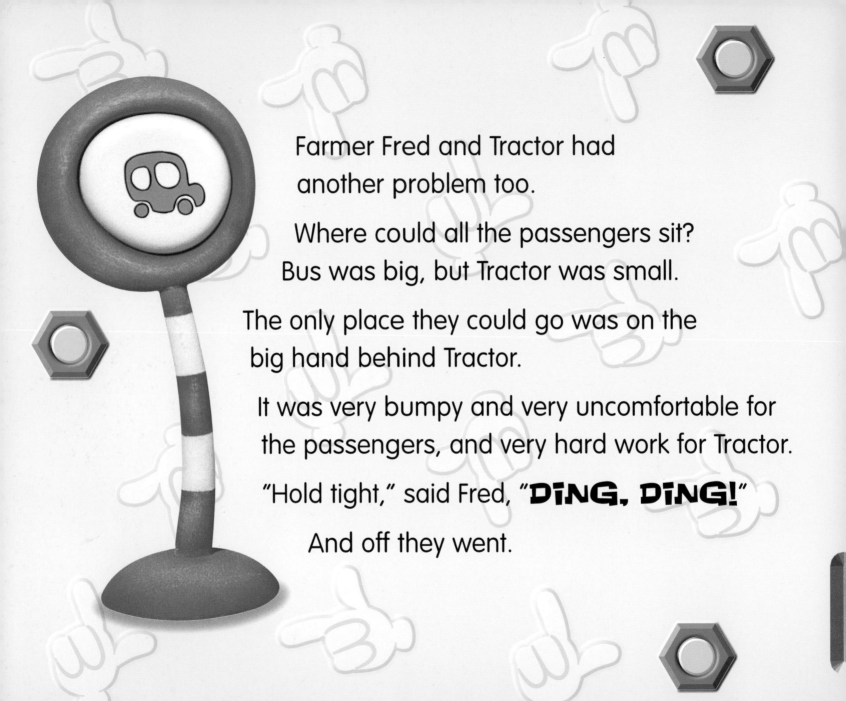

Farmer Fred and Tractor had another problem too.

Where could all the passengers sit? Bus was big, but Tractor was small.

The only place they could go was on the big hand behind Tractor.

It was very bumpy and very uncomfortable for the passengers, and very hard work for Tractor.

"Hold tight," said Fred, "**DING, DING!**"

And off they went.

Driver Dottie and Farmer Fred met in the road.

Bus was very dirty and miserable and Tractor was very tired and cross.

Engie Benjy, Jollop and Dan came zooming up.

"Hello everyone!" said Engie, "How did it go? I expect it was fun, wasn't it?"

Dottie and Fred were looking very unhappy. It had not been fun at all.

Farmer Fred's fields were a mess and Driver Dottie's passengers were upset.

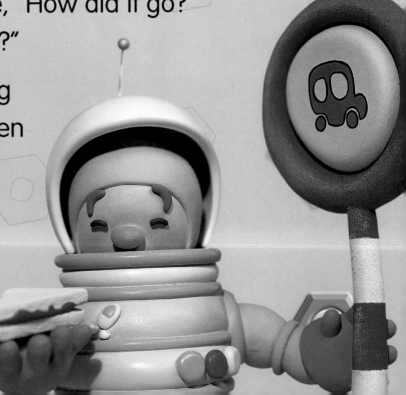

Dan handed Engie Benjy the Bus and Tractor book.

"Ah, my 'Putting Things Right with Bus and Tractor' book," said Engie.

"It says here… swapping jobs **MAY** not be as easy as it sounds, and when Bus has finished being Tractor, and Tractor has finished being Bus, you both might want to say… um… sorry?"

Farmer Fred and Driver Dottie glared at each other.

"Oh, come on, you two!" said Engie, "Farmer Fred?"

"… er… arr… Sorry," said Farmer Fred, "T'isn't easy being Bus."

"Driver Dottie?" asked Engie.

"Sorry," said Driver Dottie, "It's not easy being Tractor."

And they both shook hands, **FRIENDS AGAIN**.

"Well, team, that's alright then!" said Engie Benjy.

All the passengers cheered as Engie Benjy and Jollop zoomed off in Dan the Van.

VROOM VROOM!